Copyright and Disclaimer
Woofy Woo Woo the artist dog-©2016 Louise
Robertson Emmett
Written by Louise Elisabeth Robertson
Woofy Woo Woo Copyright © 2016 Louise
Robertson Emmett
Illustrated by Dionesia Nadya Dewayani
Edited by: DogEarPublishing
Graphic design by: Dionesia Nadya Dewayani ISBN:
978-1-45754801-7
Copyright Registration Number: 284700643

TalesILove.com
2016
First Edition

the artist dog
Woofy Woo Woo

Tales of Woofy Woo Woo ©

Written by
Louise Elisabeth Robertson

Illustrated by
Dionesia Nadya Dewayani

For my lovely Husband Frank who enjoys
my quirkiness and for Malcolm and Eileen
and of course Oscar ... They are all
inspiration to me.
All My Love !!

Woofy Woo Woo lived with two artists. One was a painter and one was a designer. They lived together as a family in a rambling Victorian house in London.

Eileen always wore black clothes and floaty, multi-coloured scarfs. Malcolm always wore creams and browns and was very neat and tidy.

2

Eileen was a painter and sometimes a printer. She had a studio full of art stuff and a very strange and large printing contraption.

3

In Eileen's art studio there were brushes, ink rollers, canvases, and tubes of different-coloured paints. Woofy loved the paints. They seemed to be all the colours of the rainbow and more! Stuff was piled high, with baskets everywhere full of ink, charcoal, and other drawing things.

Eileen would say, "Don't touch the paints Woofy!"

Eileen's studio was a little topsy-turvy, but she liked it that way!

Malcolm, the designer, had an office that was neat and tidy. His desk was extremely ordered... His paper, pens, pencils, and rulers were all organised in their different colours and shades and were kept in strict piles by his computer. There was never a mess.

Malcolm would say, "Don't touch the pens Woofy!"
Malcolm's office was always neat and tidy, but he liked it
that way!

6

Woofy Woo Woo loved his life at the house. There were always interesting people coming to view the wonderful works of art Malcolm and Eileen had made.

Eileen would say things like, "I need to get peppermint tea in, as Pete the fashion designer is coming to work on a project today" and "Frank is popping in to buy one of my paintings and he does like a cappuccino."

Woofy Woo Woo loved Eileen and Malcom very much indeed, but he had his best times with Malcolm when they went to the park together.

9

Whenever Malcolm mentioned going for a walk, Woofy would bound to the front door, sometimes slipping, sliding, and crashing on the wooden floor, all in his eagerness to go to the park. Woofy could not wait for their walk; it was his special time with Malcolm.

Woofy was an all-weather dog. He enjoyed all the different seasons of the year, rain or shine. As Woofy was the dog of artists, he especially noticed the change in colours, tones, and shades each season.

Springtime was great, as the showers made the days brighter and fresher. Malcolm tried to get Woofy to put on his smart, waterproof dog coat, but that did not always happen!

Playing ball in the park was crazy fun. Woofy would chase after the ball and end up right in the middle of the bright, golden daffodils. He liked how they nodded their heads in the wind as if they were saying hello.

In summer, Woofy Woo Woo strolled round the park with the warm sun on his back, and Malcolm was always there of course! Woofy would get excited and jump about when he saw the children running around, playing football on the grass and hopscotch in the playground. He wanted to get involved in the games too!

Woofy Woo Woo loved watching the children play.
He thought their crazy-coloured clothes were amazing.
Woofy enjoyed seeing the pinks, crimsons, oranges,
indigos, turquoises, and greens. He was an artist dog.

In autumn, Woofy Woo Woo absolutely relished his walks with Malcolm, especially when Malcolm did STICK THROWING. It was super cool when Malcolm threw the stick into a huge pile of brown and yellow leaves.

CRUNCH, CRUNCH! Woofy loved the sound and feel of the leaves as he searched wildly for the stick. Sometimes he would emerge from the leaves with an even bigger stick than he started with, almost too big to carry! As Woofy was an artist dog, he also admired the colours of autumn leaves, which were brown, red, amber, and yellow.

16

In winter, Woofy was not so keen on walks, particularly on freezing cold and icy days. But when the snow came, he had a wonderful time. Woofy tried to eat the snow, and it made him sneeze.

Woofy giggled to himself when he saw the snowmen the children had built. The snowmen had black coal eyes, orange carrot noses, and fancy hats and scarves. They brightened up the wintery days.

One of Woofy Woo Woo's favourite things to do was watching Eileen paint. He was a very observant dog and he liked watching Eileen squidge out the paint and energetically spread and brush it onto canvases or her printing contraptions.

Eileen would say, "Don't touch the paints Woofy!"

Watching Malcolm design was different. Malcolm made crisp and sharp straight-lined pictures.

Malcolm would say, "Don't touch the pens Woofy! "

Woofy sat in his special tartan dog bed, longing to make beautiful pictures just like Malcolm and Eileen.

One day Malcolm and Eileen went out. They were going to an important place that they always talked about. It sounded very grand.

Woofy Woo Woo imagined that it was where the Queen painted, as it was called the Royal Academy of Arts. Woofy thought it would be fun to go and see the Queen doing some paintings one day.

Woofy lay half snoozing in his tartan bed in the art studio. Out of the corner of his eye, he could see into Malcolm's office. As usual his pens were neat and tidy in a row.

"Don't touch the pens" thought Woofy.

Over in the art studio, Woofy spotted Eileen's paint.

"Don't touch the paints" thought Woofy.

He loved looking at that squidgy, colourful paint, and wanted to touch it to see what it felt like. He thought no one would notice, and anyway Malcolm and Eileen had left him all alone. He was bored!

Woofy climbed onto Eileen's chair and with a great leap he jumped up onto the desk and knocked a basket of paint tubes down onto a large sheet of paper. The paper was propped up by the side of the desk, and it started to fall!

Eileen had been so busy lately that she had not put the lids on the paint tubes properly, and as they hit the floor, the lids shot off. The crashing and bashing gave Woofy a fright, so he leapt off the desk and...

26

Unfortunately, he landed on the tubes, and the lovely squishy paint shot out all over the special and expensive artists paper! Then, things got worse... Woofy had managed to tread in the paint, and his paws were covered in red, blue, green, and yellow!

Woofy Woo Woo loved the feeling of the soft, squishy paint between his toes, as well as the feel of the lovely rough paper on his paws. One paw after another, he padded on the paper, returning to the squidgy paint to get some more. He was loving life and could not stop! A little more red here, a bit more blue there. This "paw painting" was great fun!

Suddenly, Woofy heard the front door opening. He looked down at his paws. EEK! He looked at his paint-splodged, glossy grey coat. AHHH! He looked at the paw print-covered paper. WHOOPS! Woofy Woo Woo did not know what to do! What he did know was that he was in BIG trouble. Or so he thought...

Eileen and Malcolm walked into the art studio, looking for Woofy Woo Woo—he had not come to the door wildly wagging his tail to greet them like he normally did.

What a sight met their eyes! Woofy thought they would be horrified—wouldn't you? But artists usually see the beauty in the world, and Woofy's first painting certainly was beautiful to Eileen and Malcolm.

"You are an artist dog for sure, Woofy Woo Woo," they cried.

Eileen picked up Woofy Woo Woo and gave him a hug.
Malcolm hugged him too, and it was one big family hug.
Then Eileen and Malcolm looked at each other and laughed.
They were both covered in multi-coloured dog prints.

Woofy Woo Woo had become an artist dog without realising it! In fact, Eileen and Malcolm adored Woofy Woo Woo's paw painting so much that they exhibited it in the local park at the Summer Artists Show.

All the children loved Woofy Woo Woo's paw painting too.
They thought it was GENIUS and AWESOME...it was
PAW-SOME. Because it was the best paw painting they
had ever seen, the children gave Woofy a special award—
The Greatest Artist Dog in the World.

Woofy Woo Woo is now an official dog artist. If you ever see
his painting, look very carefully at the bottom and you can
see where he signed his work: W.W.W. (Woofy Woo Woo).

Louise E Robertson (FRSA, MSc, B'Ed, PGC) Born in Northamptonshire UK. Louise is a successful educator, and has been a Head Teacher in three schools. As leader of leadership teams in schools in England, Scotland and Indonesia, she has always loved books for children. Louise currently lives between the UK and the USA, and is now writing for children. She is married to Frank and between them they have 6 children.

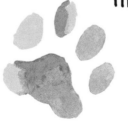

Dionesia Nadya Dewayani is studying illustration in Savannah College of Art and Design (SCAD). Born and raised in Indonesia, she fell in love with drawing as a kid and still feel like one every time she draws.

9 781457 548017